I0535095

Ascent to Easter

Mbokodo Publishers and Chuck Stephens

Published by Mbokodo Publishers, 2024.

ASCENT TO EASTER

First edition. February 12, 2024.

Copyright © 2024 Mbokodo Publishers and Chuck Stephens.

ISBN: 978-1998971411

Written by Mbokodo Publishers and Chuck Stephens.

ASCENT TO EASTER

Fragments on the Roots and Relevance of Easter

Chuck Stephens

1

Ascent to Easter

© 2024 Mbokodo Publishers

ISBN-13: 978-1-998971-41-1 (Paperback)

ISBN-13: 978-1-998971-58-0 (eBook)

Pictures credit: www.clipart-library.com

Typeset in 10/14 Garamond by Mbokodo Publishers

Printed by Mbokodo Publishers 1 2 3 4 5 1 2

Preamble

Don't look for a plot or thesis in what follows. These are snapshots of ascent up a holy mountain – one which can be metaphorical as well as geographical; and of a six-and-a-half-week period in the calendar. They are selected and recorded only to add value to your "ascent to Easter." It is a kind of virtual pilgrimage, nothing more. No certificate on completion. Virtue is its own reward.

Pilgrimages start somewhere and go somewhere. Were the Canterbury Tales starting in Canterbury or going there? It doesn't really matter because the journey will be as well remembered as the destination. Take your time. Put the book down on the coffee table and pick it up when you have time to read another chapter. Don't just read. Illustrations are provided for meditation. This journey is not an unfamiliar one. But along the way; there are nuances and some thought-provoking content that add value to what you already remember.

For your ease of reading, where websites are quoted, website text is italicized. This guide is devotional not academic, so sources are not foot-noted. Just note that some content is found through research and then borrowed.

1. Melchizadek's Mountain

Mount Moria has acquired an aura of sanctity and is the subject of many traditions. Indeed, its sacred status may date back to the early Canaanite period, when it perhaps was the cultic center of "El Elyon," God of Melchizedek, king of Salem.

In Genesis 14:18 it is recorded: "And Melchizedek, king of Salem, brought out bread and wine; he was a priest of God Most High [=El Elyon]. He blessed him, saying, Blessed be Abram of God Most High, creator of heaven and earth."

Of course, Salem became Jerusalem. It was on Mount Moriah. The annexation of Zion, another mountain just to the southwest across the Tyropoeon Valley came much later.

Did you ever wonder what language Abram and Melchizedek communicated in? Or did they use interpreters? The Hebrew language was still a long way off, it only emerged centuries later. Abraham was probably an Acadian speaker, coming from Ur. But Melchizedek?

4

Some analysts believe that Melchizedek (= the king of righteousness) was really Shem - because Abraham tithed to him. Or one of his descendants.

Abraham probably left Ur as a climate refugee. That city was dying from climate change. He was looking for greener pastures – agriculturally and metaphorically as well. He and his family did not travel from Ur to Palestine directly. First, they went upstream towards the headwaters of the two rivers (remember that "Mesopotamia" means the land between the rivers – both of which rise in High Armenia.) Specifically, to Haran. One day, Abraham would send his majordomo Eliezar back to Haran to find a suitable wife for his only son Isaac.

But after his father Terah died (in Haran) Abraham decided to move south west around the so-called "fertile crescent." A distant relative of his had already blazed the trail. His name was Eber. That name means "the region beyond." *Eber could refer to both the person and to the region where he settled. This also happened in the case of two other descendents of Shem – Arphaxad and Serug. These are both names of districts (even in present-day Turkey) as well as of individuals.*

The word "Hebrew" is a derivative of Eber's name. But as Abraham was but a distant relative of his, the name Hebrew probably designated the region as opposed to the person. Eber was a great-grandson of Shem, one of Noah's sons. Noah's ark had landed on Mount Ararat, from where his family moved gradually downriver. Eber remained in the region hosting his great grandfather Shem somewhere near Salem. According to Sefer Ha Yashar (Jasher), this was at Moriah. He was greeted. This explains why the patriarchs were known as "sons of Eber." In the genealogy of the Semites, Abraham and, especially, Israel are called descendants of "Eber." The affiliation was with both a relative and with a place – "a region beyond."

Between Noah and Eber were: Shem, Arphaxad, Cainan and Selah – five generations.

Abraham was Terah's son. Terah was Nahor's son. Nahor was Serug's son. Serug was Reu's son. Reu was Peleg's son. Peleg was Eber's son. So,

Abraham was only a distant relative of Eber's. However, Eber lived long. He out-lived both Terah and Abraham. He lived well into the life of Isaac and even into Jacob's lifetime. He taught them all the ways of the Lord, which explains why they were called Hebrews.

Here is a useful timeline that aligns with both Genesis and Jasher:

Year (AM)	Family news
2003	Abram goes to Canaan without Lot and Eber is already in Canaan
2018	In Canaan Abram receives the promise he will inherit the land at the age of 70 while in Canaan. He returns to Haran to his family
2023	He returns to Canaan, after 5 years, with Lot and a large entourage from Haran
2048	Eber and Shem and the great people of the land celebrate the birth of Isaac
2083	Terah dies in Haran, in Isaac's 35th year
2085	Isaac is offered to God at his 37th year at Moriah (where Eber lives) and Sarah dies at the age of 127. Isaac goes to Eber and Shem to be trained
2088	Isaac returns to Beersheba to Abraham
2096	Arphaxad dies when Isaac is 48
2108	Jacob and Esau are born
2126	Shelah dies when Isaac is 78 and Jacob's 18th year, he is sent for 32 years to Eber to be trained in the ways of the Lord
2158	Shem dies in the 110th year of Isaac, when Jacob is 50 and Jacob returns to Isaac at Hebron
2187	Eber dies when Jacob is 79 during his second year with Laban in Paddan Haran

"Semitic" languages are those descended from Noah's son Shem. The proliferation of languages occurred after the flood, above all as God's response to the Tower of Babel. So, it is unlikely that the same Acadian language that Abraham grew up with in Ur (where Sumerian was also common) was in common usage when he migrated to Canaan. Language study would have been familiar to Abraham, also as he wandered into Egypt for a time. He would have been bi-lingual in Ur and perhaps multi-lingual in his new setting. It is possible that Shem – who lived long – could remember the pre-Flood or "Adamic" language? Perhaps this was one thing that he taught to his many descendents? Aramaic is sometimes thought to be a very ancient language, perhaps it is a variant of the ancestral language that served as a *lingua franca* for the royal line?

An African aside

By Princess Adeshua Abosede Ya'Aruba:

It is so unfortunate that people that are interpreting the Talmud didn't speak Aramaic language. The Yoroubawa that the Bible was written in their language are still in Nigeria. The language is presently called the Niger Congo language. Eber ah Nahar simply means our Father Noah or Nuwa. The last Israelite king DhuNuwas who was persecuted from Yemen in 525 AD did not sink into the Red Sea. He went to Ile Ife in Nigeria to establish another kingdom that Nuwabi/Yoruba/Oduah in Nigeria, Togo and Benin republic. The Yoruba were formerly called Yeruba. But they are now called Yoruba the short form of Yoroubawa/Yoroubara/Yoroibara.

2. A Centenarian's love-child

It is a well-known story, how Abraham and Sarah became parents to Isaac at an advanced age. He was more than a "late lamb," he was a walking miracle.

In Genesis 22, God commands Abraham, "Take now your son, your only son, whom you love, Isaac, and go to the land of Moriah, and offer him there as a burnt offering on one of the mountains which I will tell you" (Genesis 22:2).

The place God led Abraham was Mount Moriah. This was the mountain where Eber and Melchizadek lived. Abraham didn't fully understand what God was asking him to do in light of God's previous promise to establish an everlasting covenant with Isaac (Genesis 17:19); nonetheless, he trusted God and by faith offered Isaac as a sacrifice. Of course, God intervened and spared Isaac's life by providing a ram instead. Abraham thereafter called this place "The LORD Will Provide. And to this day it is said, 'On the mountain of the LORD it will be provided'" (Genesis 22:14).

Because of Abraham's obedience on Mount Moriah, God told Abraham that his "descendants will take possession of the cities of their enemies, and through your offspring all nations on earth will be blessed because you have obeyed me" (Genesis 22: 17, 18).

Abraham's life story starts in Ur and ends in Hebron, south of Jerusalem. He bought a burial site there from the local people, and this has come to be the second holiest site in Judaism, second only to the Temple Mount. There were apparently oaks or terebinth trees standing at Hebron or Mamre at the time. Climate change continues to pursue Abraham long after his death, because in this setting today, you can hardly even find a blade of grass.

So, although Abraham visited Mount Moriah more than once, he did not occupy it. As the children of Israel occupied the promised land

and gradually conquered it, Mounts Zion and Moriah would remain in Jebusite hands until the time of King David.

3. Mount Moria

The tradition of "Jacob's Dream" is also identified with Mount Moriah: "He came upon a certain place and stopped there for the night, for the sun had set. Taking one of the stones of that place, he put it under his head and lay down in that place. He had a dream; a stairway was set on the ground and its top reached to the sky, and angels of God were going up and down on it. And the Lord was standing beside him... Jacob awoke from his sleep and said. . . "How awesome is this place! This is none other than the abode of God and that is the gateway to heaven" (Genesis 28:10-18).

This is perhaps the most colourful representation of the essential nature of the site which some would later claim was the "navel of the world." At the summit of Mount Moriah, traditionally, is the "Foundation Stone," the symbolic fundament of the world's creation, and reputedly the site of the Temple's Holy of Holies.

Mountains are rich in symbolism perhaps because of the military advantage that they offered in the days of walled cities and siege warfare. (Think Masada.) Thus, you get expressions like *"the moral high ground... a mountain-top experience... on the up-and-up..."* and so on.

11

To the Greeks, Mount Olympus was the home of the gods. To the Hebrews, Mount Sinai was where God wrote the Ten Commandments onto two tablets. From Mount Nebo east of the Jordan, Moses was able to look into the Promised Land although he would not live to enter it himself.

Mount Moriah is the name of the elongated north-south stretch of land lying between the Kidron Valley to the east and the Tyropoeon Valley to the west. Mount Zion stands south-west of Mount Moriah, and is slightly taller in elevation. The Mount of Olives lies to the east of the Kidron valley. Sprawling over these mountains is now the city of Jerusalem.

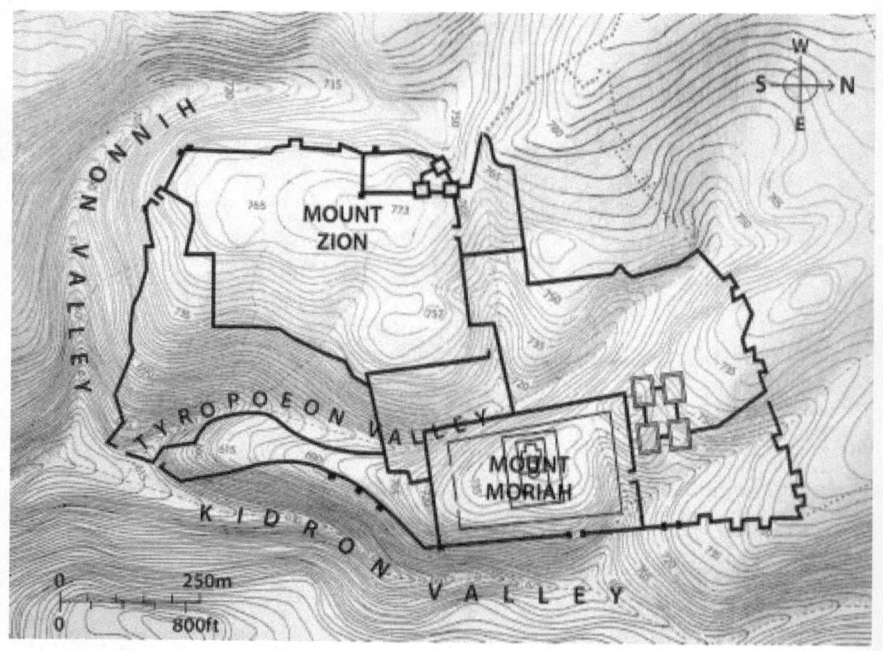

Source: Jerusalem360. com

4. The Temple Mount

About a thousand years after Abraham climbed that mountain with his only son Isaac at this very location... King David captured the citadel of Zion from the Jebusites. Then he expanded his capital to include both Mount Zion and Mount Moriah, and named it for himself – the city of David.

The Jebusite "Zion" was situated above the Gihon Spring. To the north, Mount Moria's summit lay desolate for long after Zion's capture by David. It was in fact still the private property of Araunah, the city's former Jebusite king. For various reasons David did not confiscate the site but preferred to buy it from Auranah for full value: "So David paid Ornan (Auranah) for the site 600 shekels' worth of gold. And David built there an altar to the Lord and sacrificed burnt offerings and offerings of well-being" (I Chronicles 21:25, and a slightly different version at II Samuel 24:18-25).

King David bought the threshing floor of Arauna the Jebusite and built an altar to the Lord so that a "plague may be held back from the people." After David's death, his son King Solomon built a glorious temple on the same site – the citadel. The consecutive reigns of David and Solomon were the golden age of Israel.

Solomon's temple lasted for over four hundred years until it was destroyed by King Nebuchadnezzar's armies in 587/586 B. C. Upon the completion of the first Temple, famed for its sumptuous splendour, the Ark of the Covenant was placed within its confines. The sanctity of the site is reflected in the graphic description provided by the Book of Kings: "the priests came out of the sanctuary for the cloud had filled the House of the Lord and the priests were not able to remain and perform the service because of the cloud, for the Presence of the Lord filled the House of the Lord. . . " (I Kings 8:11).

Solomon built his palace in the "miloh" (infill) area which separated the summit of the mountain and the Temple from the city below. This was also a concrete expression of the divine inspiration that was attributed to

13

his kingship. Other palaces were also built nearby, such as the "House of the Forest of Lebanon" and the House of Pharaoh's Daughter. Solomon used dirt to fill in this east-west lateral rift, hence the area's name: "miloh" (infill), or Ophel, from a Hebrew word referring to the road that ascended to the Temple from the city which at that time was topographically lower.

Seventy years later the temple was rebuilt on the same site by the Jews who returned to Jerusalem following their Babylon captivity. Around the first century, King Herod made a significant addition to this second Temple structure, which then came to be known as Herod's Temple. It was this temple that Jesus cleansed in John 2:15.

However, in A. D. 70, the Roman armies led by Titus, son of the Emperor Vespasian, once again destroyed the temple. All that remains of the Temple Mount of that era is a portion of a retaining wall known as the "Western Wall" or the "Wailing Wall." It has been a destination for pilgrims and a site of prayer for Jews for many centuries.

The God who first called Abraham to Mount Moriah still has plans for this holy place. The Bible indicates that a third temple will be built on or near the site of Solomon's temple (Daniel 9:27). This would seem to present a problem given the political obstacles that stand in the way: the religious activities on the Temple Mount are currently controlled by the Supreme Muslim Council (the Waqf). Yet nothing can put a wrinkle in God's sovereign plans. Thus, Muslim control of this area simply fulfils the prophecy of Luke 21:24 that "Jerusalem will be trampled on by the Gentiles until the times of the Gentiles are fulfilled. "

Sitting atop Mount Moriah today is the Temple Mount, a 37-acre tract of land where the Jewish temple once stood. Three important Islamic holy sites are there now, including the Dome of the Rock, the Dome of the Chain and the Al-Aqsa Mosque – Muslim shrines all built around thirteen hundred years ago.

The spiritual importance of Jerusalem in Islam is further emphasized due to its status as the first Qibla (direction of prayer). Islamic tradition holds that Muhammad led prayers towards Jerusalem until the 16th or

17th month after his migration from Mecca to Medina, when Allah directed him to instead turn towards the Kaaba in Mecca. Jerusalem's significance and holiness to Muslims also derives from its strong association with Abraham, David, Solomon and Jesus – all of whom are all regarded as prophets of Islam. Their stories are all mentioned in the Qur'an.

In Sunni Islam, Jerusalem is the third-holiest city after Mecca and Medina. Muslims believe that Muhammad was transported to Jerusalem during his Night Journey (Isra and Mi'raj). The Qur'an describes how the prophet was taken by the miraculous steed Buraq from the Great Mosque of Mecca to the Al-Aqsa Mosque ("the farthest place of prayer") where he prayed, and then to visit heaven in a single night in the year 610.

The question has to be asked if there is not enough room on this citadel for two monotheist religions to co-habitate?

5. Carnival

All religions calendarize certain rituals, feasts and festivals. As Christianity emerged out of Judaism, it is fair to say that there are many parallels between Jewish Passover and Christian Easter.

Another common spiritual discipline is a pilgrimage. Jerusalem certainly became the centre of annual pilgrimage during the eras of the two temples. Later in history, it became a focal point for longer pilgrimages – like Rome and Mecca. Visiting Mecca is still very much a part of recommended practice for Muslims.

All cultures have spring festivals and harvest feasts. Summer and winter solstices are also celebrated widely. The thing is, though, that spring in New Orleans is harvest time in Rio de Janeiro. So as Christianity spread out around the globe, it adopted uniform festivals that commemorated events in the life of Jesus. For example, Christmas celebrates his birth – the Incarnation. But the timing of this festival is probably syncretistic – perhaps borrowed from the Roman festival of Saturnalia (celebrated at winter solstice). In the northern hemisphere, that is not a time of year when shepherds would be out "in the fields abiding." You can't have one date for Christmas in the global north and another in the global south.

The same happened to Easter, which is closely associated with the Passover feast in Judaism. In the Jewish calendar, Passover always falls on the 15th day of Nisan. But unlike Christmas (25 December every year) the date of Easter varies.

The church adopted a 40-day period called Lent to precede Easter. This relates to the 40 days that Jesus fasted in the wilderness at the beginning of his ministry. It is a season of self-denial. That could explain the name of Carnival, derived from two Latin words *carnis* (meat) and *levare* (leave off). Customarily, no meat was eaten during Lent. Perhaps only fish? However, Carnival itself has become very "carnal."

16

Somehow, the introduction of Lent called for a huge party just before entering into this long period of self-denial in the run-up to Holy Week. (For every action, there is an equal and opposite reaction.)As sexual desires were also to be suppressed during Lent, Carnival was a time to let loose, promiscuously.

One cannot rule out a little syncretism in Carnival as well, perhaps scheduled at the time of the spring equinox. *The spring festival of Ishtar in Babylon, or Osiris in Egypt signalled new birth. Another pre-spring festival was celebrated in the middle of these two known as the "love-fest" of Lupercalia. Could this be the origin of our Valentine's Day? Nerthus the fertility goddess was at the centre of these celebrations, driving out winter and making sure that fertility would return in the spring.*

Napoleon abolished Venice Carnival in 1797. It was finally brought back in 1979. It is a city-wide masquerade party. Masks from all over the world crowd the Venetian squares, but above all St Mark's square and its cafes. Besides the traditional masks you can see queer and quaint disguises. There are many dances, parties, concerts and performances in theatres. On the last day, out of respect for tradition, the image of Carnival is burnt in St Mark's square. In Brazil, Carnival features parades and 24/7 partying. It is hard to see the connection to Christian behaviour any more. It has become very secularized. To the extent that some Christians even boycott Carnival.

Unlike Lent and Holy Week, the length of Carnival is a bit elastic – it varies from place to place and from time to time. In 1991, Carnival was cancelled because of the Gulf War. In 2013, there was a heavy snowfall, causing it to be suspended for a day. And in 2020 during the Covid-19 crisis, it was cancelled early – as it proved to be a super-spreader.

But you cannot cancel either Lent or Easter.

6. Pancake Tuesday

Shrove Tuesday or "Mardi Gras" is the last day of Carnival. The name Shrove comes from the old middle English word "Shriven" meaning to go to confession to say sorry for the things you've done wrong. *Lent always starts on a Wednesday, so people went to confessions on the day before. This became known as Shriven Tuesday and then later as Shrove Tuesday. To be "shriven" meant to be absolved.*

Confession is always followed by absolution, and sometimes by penance. So, Lent can also be seen as an annual discipline of penance. Along with its celebration of feasting, another tradition of Shrove Tuesday includes Christians repenting of their sins in preparation to start the season of Lent. Ælfric of Eynsham's[1] Ecclesiastical Institutes from about 1000 AD declared: "In the week immediately before Lent everyone shall go to his confessor and confess his deeds and the confessor shall so shrive him as he then may hear by his deeds what he is to do" (i. e. in the way of penance).

The other name for this day, Pancake Day, comes from the old English custom of using up all the fattening ingredients in the house before Lent, so that people were ready to fast during Lent. The fattening ingredients that most people had in their houses in those days were eggs and milk. A very simple recipe to use up these ingredients was to combine them with some flour and make pancakes!

---

1.   *https://en.wikipedia.org/wiki/%C3%86lfric_of_Eynsham*

In French, "Mardi Gras" means "Fat Tuesday" and also comes from the idea of using up food before Lent. Mardi Gras arrived in the United States as a small festival marking French explorers Sieur de Bienville and Pierre Le Moyne d'Iberville's landing at what is now New Orleans, Louisiana on March 3, 1699.

While the dates of Easter vary from year to year, one factor is fixed. Shrove Tuesday falls forty-seven days before Easter.

A bell would be rung to call people to confession, which became known as the "Pancake Bell" and it is still rung today. Some churches also burn the palms distributed during the previous year's Palm Sunday liturgies to make the ashes used during the services held on the very next day, Ash Wednesday.

Many Christians conclude their determination of what Lenten sacrifices they will make for the 40 days of Lent on Shrove Tuesday. While undergoing a Lenten sacrifice, it is helpful to pray for strength; and encouraging fellow Christians in their fast saying, for example: "May God bless your Lenten sacrifice. "

Before the Christian era, the Slavs believed that the change of seasons was a struggle between Jarilo, the god of vegetation, fertility and springtime, and the evil spirits of cold and darkness, and that they had to help Jarilo in his worthy efforts. The whole celebration of the arrival of spring lasted a week and a large part of this was making and eating pancakes. The hot, round pancakes symbolised the sun and the Slavs believed that by eating pancakes, they got the power, light and warmth of the sun.

In all of these festivals there may be a pinch of syncretism. But that does not rob them of their authenticity.

7. Ash Wednesday

On the first day of Lent, also known as the Day of Ashes, Christians would traditionally attend mass to have a small cross of ashes drawn on their forehead by the priest. The cross is in reference to the Biblical passage "For dust you are and to dust you shall return" (Genesis 3:19).

However, neither Carnival nor Lent have much to do with Passover. There was no such period of preparation in Judaism. These tend to be medieval customs arising from European culture.

This day is to focus the Christian's heart on repentance and prayer, usually through personal and communal confession. That usually involves going to church. The mood is solemn - many services will have long periods of silence and worshipers will often leave the service in silence. No matter whether confession is spoken to a priest or directly to God in silent prayer, the point is repentance. "Confession is good for the soul."

The cross on the forehead and benediction quoted above (Genesis 3:19) follows.

As fasting rules have been relaxed in recent decades, Ash Wednesday along with Good Friday remain as days when fasting is still practiced. The calendar calculations evolved a bit over the centuries, but ended up with 40 days prior to Holy Week.

So, Ash Wednesday is 46 days before Easter – it is the last festival date on the calendar before Palm Sunday. However, for some Christians (most of whom are Roman Catholics, without suggesting that all Catholics think so...) Holy Week begins two days before Palm Sunday on the Friday of Sorrows. But Protestants like me tend to play down events that are centred on Mary. That Friday feast was a liturgical feast called the Seven Sorrows of Mary. I just mention it in passing, out of respect for that tradition. It falls just two days before Palm Sunday.

8. Lent

*The first records of the word Lent come from before 900. It comes **from the Old English word læncte**, meaning "lengthening (of daylight hours)" (or, less literally, "spring" or "springtime").* Put another way, this means that Lent is never mentioned in scripture. So those Christians who espouse a "*sola scriptura*" tend to ignore it.

Whereas other feasts and festivals may contain a pinch of syncretism, Lent is more biblically based. As noted above, it was practiced from the earliest period of Christian history, even though not labelled. It is a case of the imitation of Christ.

Although Lent was not formalized in the Christian calendar until after the Council of Nicea, St. Irenaeus, Pope St. Victor I, and St. Athanasius all seem to have written about Lent during their ministries. So, it was being observed informally when the church was underground.

Great faith leaders like John the Baptist and Jesus of Nazareth did observe varying lengths of time alone in the wilderness. Today this may be practiced by hiking or canoeing, or by just receding into the quiet of your home for prayer and meditation.

In medieval times, people took penance much more seriously than they do now. For example – fasting. The whole of Lent would be a fast in those days, that this is still observed in the Eastern Orthodox church. For example, during Lent in Ethiopia, Coptic Christians will only take one meal a day – in the evening. And what they can eat at those meals is limited by customs. Self-denial is a spiritual discipline. Today it tends to come out as diets or charitable giving, not as fasting.

The period of 40 days of Lent ends as Holy Week begins.

9. Palm Sunday

For most of us, Holy Week begins with Palm Sunday, otherwise known as Passion Sunday.

A close look at the four gospels that tell the story variously turned up a few reminders:

- Luke's account says that Jesus visited Jericho on his way up to Jerusalem for the Passover feast. That is when he met with Zachaeus, perhaps the week before?
- John's account of Mary the sister of Lazarus and Martha breaking open the alabaster jar and anointing his feet with very expensive spikenard ointment says that this happened six days before Passover. Assuming that Passover began on Good Friday, this would be the previous Saturday, presumably at night (the Sabbath ends at sundown). So that is the evening before the triumphal entry into Jerusalem
- During this whole festival, Jesus enjoyed the hospitality of this family in Bethany. All through the week he travelled in the morning from Bethany over the Mount of Olives down into Jerusalem. The first time he did this was on a "colt" (Synoptic gospels) or an "ass" (John's gospel) – that was from Bethany. As he descended into Jerusalem on that day (the first day of the week, the day after the Sabbath), he was met with adulation

Palm Sunday was the day when the arrival of Jesus was celebrated by the Jews who welcomes him as a prophet – from Galilee. It is doubtful that Pilate was met with such acclaim amidst the gloom of Roman occupation and oppression, when he arrived on his annual visit from his sea-side capital at Caesarea-Maritima. Jesus was a popular figure and the latent nationalism of the Jews thus rose to dangerous proportions. Clearly this spooked the Romans, who remained edgy all through the

Passover festival. Both palm branches and olive branches are still used for worship on this Sunday, recalling the public welcome that Jesus received as he rode into the city. But he did not ride into the city on a white steed. I think that donkeys also have colts?

That reminds me of Harry Kemp's poem:
I saw the conquerors riding by, with cruel lips and faces wan
Musing on kingdoms sacked and burned, there rode the Mongol, Genghis Khan
And Alexander, like a god, who sought to weld the world in one
And Caesar with his laurel wreath, and like a thing from hell, the Hun
And leading – like a star – the van, heedless of upstretched arm and groan
Inscrutable Napoleon went, dreaming of empire, and alone
Then all they perished from the earth, like fading shadows from a glass
And conquering down the centuries came Christ - the swordless - on an ass

Jesus was the king of the Jews. He did conquer – in an unexpected way. Every year, we welcome him back into our midst, on the first day of the week (a Sunday) that leads into Passover (the 15th of Nisan).

May he keep invading your city and your life - with his prophetic teachings and values.

10. Maundy Monday

When I hear these words together, I always think of the Mamas and the Papas song – Maundy Monday.

On his way to the temple that day, Jesus was hungry and approached a fig tree to pick some fruit. He found it bearing no fruit and cursed it. The next day, his disciples noted that the tree had withered.

Every day that week, Jesus went to the temple. On the Monday, he drove the gold-diggers out of the temple. Some were merchants, some were money changers. He declared that his father's house was a place for prayer, not for business. This prompted some questions about his legitimacy. Questioning his authoritycould have been a trap, trying to capture him in making claims that could lead to accusations of blasphemy?

Remember, to the Jews, these were all week-days. Even Sunday was not their Sabbath. Jesus was "at work", and in Jerusalem at the time of a festival, that took him straight to the temple. He spoke truth to power. And he engaged their questions about his spiritual authority. He taught multitudes of people. Many parables are recorded during this Holy Week as well as his debates with religious leaders.

Then every evening, it was back over the Mount of Olives to his lodgings in Bethany. I doubt that Lazarus went to the temple every day, as he was a well-to-do businessman. Maybe he had an olive press, living so close to the Mount of Olives? Maybe he exported olives? Not everyone who reads this will frequent a place of worship like Jesus did. It doesn't matter. Just be sure to welcome him into your home, and into your heart. Jesus and Lazarus were very close friends. In fact, "the city was stirred" on Palm Sunday because of the reputation Jesus had won for himself by calling forth Lazarus from his grave, on an earlier visit to Bethany.

11. Maundy Tuesday

The word "maundy" comes from the Latin "mandatum" for commandment. I am familiar with this from my Portuguese – "mandar" is to command. The common people who didn't speak Latin heard it regularly as a chant at the foot washing, so eventually it became "the maundy" for them.

Each morning as Jesus and his entourage trod over the Mount of Olives, Jerusalem would come into full view before him. His laments for the city, and what lay in store for it, were recorded during Holy Week. He seemed to understand in his own mind where the whole narrative was going.

Jesus was a teacher, a rabbi. His disciples travelled with him, sort of like a team ministry. So when he went to the temple every day in Holy Week, there were a number of witnesses who would later recall what he had taught. Maundy Tuesday began with a major debate between him and the religious leaders, prompted by the activism of Maundy Monday.

His replies often came in the form of parables. It was a cunning methodology that the multitudes could understand, without him directly implicating the religious leaders. The priests and scribes came in bundles – like Pharisees and Sadducees, each with their own theological nuances. He and his disciples were another bundle. The multitudes could listen in to the debate, and decide for themselves.

Recently, the Vatican suspended the custom of priests saying individual masses in side-altars around St Peter's Basilica. They say that it suddenly went very quiet, as that rule came into effect. The only comparison that I am drawing here is that in the temple, there were different strands of Judaism being preached, all around. Jesus had his own branding. That was emerging clearly and distinctly from other strands. Each rabbi could teach a cluster of listeners. This got a bit noisy.

(By the way, I usually preface any remarks that I make like this with an admission that I am not an RC. But I try to give "equal time" to diverse theologies. I mentioned that the feast of the Seven Sorrows of Mary precedes Holy Week. It is the Friday before Good Friday, but Holy Week proper begins with Palm Sunday.)

A lot of his teaching in Holy Week was in this "marketplace exchange of theologies." Today, we experience a lot of that "noise" on social media. Then in the evenings, in Bethany, he also told parables to those who were "at meat with him."

But by Tuesday night, the religious leaders had been upstaged by this rabbi from Galilee, to the extent that a revenging mood was setting in. His popularity was positively dangerous. He was not just a prophet and a faith-healer, but a populist too. Something had to be done to put him in his place.

12. Spy Wednesday

Over brunch on Maundy Tuesday, we were debating whether Judas was (in modern parlance) a "double-agent" or a "mole"? He is usually just called a "traitor" for betraying Jesus, but they could only arrest him safely, away from the crowds, so they needed "intel" about his movements. That is how this day got the name "Spy Wednesday."

I find this particularly detestable knowing that the State Security Agency in South Africa is used to spy on citizens – illegally. It is not part of the SSA's mandate and infringes on our right to privacy. Intel is used to extort people and to intimidate them, in many cases for the self-preservation of the perpetrators. They deserve the same fate as Judas.

With the launch of Judas' betrayal on this night, the light started to dim. So traditionally, the matins on Maundy Thursday, Good Friday and Holy Saturday lit a dwindling number of candles. It got dimmer and darker as the week went on. These liturgies are usually called the "Tenebrae" (the Latin word for darkness). Near the end of the services, the candles would be extinguished gradually, ending in total darkness. Then there would be a loud noise or "strepitus." This "service of shadows" may have alluded to the total eclipse of the sun on Good Friday, when Jesus cried out "It is finished"? But these are layered shadows:

- The shadow of betrayal
- The shadow of the agony of spirit and arrest
- The shadow of denial
- The shadow of accusation
- The shadow of crucifixion and humiliation
- The shadow of death
- The shadow of burial

All this started with betrayal, which was really ignited by an event on Wednesday night in Bethany. The synoptic gospels say that supper that night was at the home of Simon the leper. John says it was in the home of Lazarus. But both agree that it was in Bethany. John says that Jesus came to Bethany six days before Passover (i. e. which was on Good Friday). The incident that I am speaking of was the anointing of Jesus' feet with expensive spikenard. John says that it was Judas who took exception to this. However, the other three synoptic gospels say it was the disciples (Matthew), "some" (Mark) and "the Pharisees" (Luke). No matter. All agree that this is when Judas went off to see those who were clearly looking for a way to sideline this upstart Galilean prophet and faith-healer. You don't have to be a rocket scientist to realize that they wanted to silence him.

Judas started down a slippery slope, as they say. The agreement, sealed by a price to be paid in silver, was to "deliver him unto them." It sounded ominous, but what they would do, or could do, was a bit tentative. The Passover was always a turbulent festival in Jerusalem because of the animosity between Jews and Romans. There had been other Jewish heroes in the past who had succumbed to jittery Roman hegemony. But the narrative is a bit vague, about where this was all going. (Although

Jesus himself had predicted that it would not end well, so his anointing on whatever night was pretty symbolic.)

Reading John 12:1 again, I am less sure that the anointing by Mary of Bethany was the night before Palm Sunday. It does say there that he came to Bethany six days before Passover, as he begins this account of the anointing. But the logic of the narrative is clear – it was this anointing that provoked Judas into action. It was the trigger. So, it could have happened as late as the night of Spy Wednesday. He then struck a deal with the enemies of Jesus, and the shadows started to close in, layer on layer. He would provide them with "intel" so that Jesus could be "delivered" at an opportune moment, when the crowds would not be watching.

13. Maundy Thursday

This was the day of preparation for the Passover which starts at sun-down. Jesus sent Peter and John to make preparations (they both lived long enough to relate the narrative to the gospel writers). Their "booking" was in an upper room in the home of Barnabas, Mary and her son John Mark. (The same Mark who wrote one gospel, so there is a reliable source.)

Preparation that day would have involved Peter and John going to the temple with an animal sacrifice. Possibly the last one they ever made? Some blood of that sacrifice would be sprinkled on the altar, and the shank would become the centrepiece of the evening meal. Many believe that they were actually celebrating the Passover (seder) supper. Except Jesus re-invented the symbolism, changing the Passover to the Eucharist.

John's account of the foot-washing has also become a common aspect of Maundy Thursdayworship. This is commonly called the Last Supper because Jesus was soon to be delivered over to his enemies.

Reading over the events of Maundy Thursday, I do not get the impression that Jesus had "lost control" of events. He foresees who and where Peter and John can rendezvous, to book the upper room. He is not in hiding, and never was. He is right there in the temple daily, engaging the powers and the multitudes. If anything, those plotting against him are afraid that if they make their move, the people will rise to his defense. Crowd control can be very unpredictable. At the Last Supper, he is no longer a guest at the home of Lazarus or Simon the leper - he is the host. He even re-invents the symbolism, which could not have been improvised. He is aware that there is a plot to sideline him, and even who the "mole" is, dipping into the same bowl with him. Then there is this long pause on the Mount of Olives – to pray. Remember this is the night of the Passover, and Jesus prayed hard that he might be spared what he knew was coming.

In his book <u>Who Moved the Stone?</u> Frank Morison reads this long delay on the path back to Bethany as a rendezvous. Every day they had crossed over the Mount of Olives, which had two footpaths. Between these two routes was a garden called Gethsemane. How did Judas know that they would be waiting there, since he had left the Last Supper several hours earlier? Why did they stop to pray there and not just go on to Bethany? Why did such a brigade of guards arrive to arrest an unarmed rabbi, far from the madding crowd? The intel sold by Judas was not just where to go to arrest him, but that Jesus was talking openly of his demise (body broken, bloodshed, etc). This was a key factor in the decision to go ahead with his arrest and rush to trial before the sabbath arrived.

The first time that I was arrested (of three times) in September 2017, the rush was to lock me up (i. e. scare tactics). I was released the next morning by the magistrate - without bail. Then the police filibustered as long as possible to reach trial. Five months passed, and three court appearances. Legal fees rising. Then they withdrew their case, as they had no evidence to justify what they had done. Then we sued the Commissioner of Police, in February 2018. A trial date has still not been set - five years later! It took three years for us to get a look at the docket – there had been no investigation. It was just crude use of brute force. Now the state attorneys are ducking and diving about a trial date. The system still knows how to protect itself. Our police are no better than the armed guards of Caiaphas.

On this night, his enemies closed in around him. He did not resist arrest. The Sanhedrin was convened illegally – it should never meet at night. The trumped-up charges failed to stick. But he interrupted his Miranda-rights silence to confirm that he was the messiah. To the Jews, this was blasphemy - a capital offense. So, he was blindfolded, beaten and mocked. But only the Romans could execute a death sentence, so the charges were recycled - into insurrection against Caesar.

During this awful night, however, Pilate's wife Claudia had disturbing dreams. In the morning, she warned her husband against getting involved. Worst of all, Peter denied even knowing Jesus - three times - before the cock crowed at daybreak.

14. Good Friday

This day was on a time-line, so to speak. Everyone was in a hurry. Claudia was in a hurry to warn Pilate against getting involved. The Jewish leaders had only until sundown to push through a trial and a Roman execution. The Roman military had only a few hours to crucify three prisoners. The few friends that remained loyal to Jesus were in a hurry to arrange a proper burial for him before the sun set, as per Jewish custom. So, there was a sense of urgency driving all the day's events.

But it was an obstacle course. Claudia's warning caused Pilate to try to deflect the trial to Herod, the tribal leader. Jesus was tired and weak from beatings and loss of sleep and could not manage to carry his cross (read: gallows) all the way to Golgotha, along the Via Dolorosa. The population of Jerusalem always swelled for the Passover festival, so crowd-control was on everyone's mind. The Jewish authorities used this crowd factor effectively, inciting the crowd to demand the release of Barabbas instead of Jesus. Sadly, most of the cadres of Jesus had fled in fear, so they could not rally the crowds in his favour. However, one of the four gospel writers was an eye-witness himself (John).

Crowd manipulation is still with us. If anything, public opinion is feared today more than ever. We saw riots on an unprecedented scale in the USA during the Covid crisis. Riots sending messages. In South Africa, defiant leaders and ex-leaders are currently "working the crowds" to try to save themselves and their perverse views. Protesting is one thing; it is legitimate expression of civic voices. It is good citizenship. But crowds can be swayed, too. And social media has become an instrument for agitators and instigators. We are beguiled by algorithms. Surveillance videos of the riot on 6 January 2020 are inconclusive. Not all the participants were violent, and there were periods when the intrusion was calm and controlled. But there were moments of breaking and entering, which some blame on instigators rather than the mob itself. The gospels make it clear that the crowd in Jerusalem was manipulated by instigators, pushing their narrative intentionally. Crowds can be steered. In the aftermath there seems to have been exaggeration of one narrative, but the question is whether that was entrapment? The jury is still out on this episode of mob action. How violent was it? Or was it just legitimate protesting? I suspect that it was manipulated.

Further recorded obstacles on Good Friday included a solar eclipse that plunged the city into darkness for three hours. (Those of us who experience load-shedding know how interruptive sudden darkness can be.)And then an earthquake that spooked even the dead.

I admire Joseph of Arimathea and Nicodemus for coming forward to guarantee Jesus a proper burial. They had been secret admirers, because they were also respectable members of the Sanhedrin – who had opposed his conviction. They saw value in his ministry, and Joseph was actually a distant relative. So, he had grounds to request the body for burial. And he had a tomb already carved in bedrock nearby.

Can we date this fateful day? Well, the first day of Passover is always the 15th of Nisan. And there are only eleven years that Pilate was procurator of Judea. Of those eleven years, how many times did the 15th of Nisan fall on a Friday? Attempts have been made to pin down a date, using calendar converters – because the Jewish calendar is different. But other adjustments come into it, because of the "Gregorian reformation" of the calendar over a thousand years later. It's complicated.

I said that I didn't think that Jesus had "lost control" of the events of Maundy Thursday. I have the same sense as I read "the Passion." His life was not taken away from him. He gave his life, out of compassion. That is why the remembrance of his crucifixion is called the "Eucharist." That is Greek for "Thank you."

On Good Friday, the Moravians hold a love-feast, and they clean up the graves in their cemeteries.

Michael Jackson's famous music-video Thriller set records when it was released. It often reminded me that among the signs and wonders recorded in the Gospels on Good Friday – along with darkness falling at noon and a mighty earthquake - was that dead people were seen walking around. Spooky as this may seem, the word "thriller" certainly describes the events of this day and the two days that followed.

Lazarus had been a dead man walking. No wonder that the Romans put an armed guard on the tomb that was hastily loaned to Jesus. In those days, tombs were not single, but multiple. The main thing was to provide a proper Jewish burial. This did not preclude further use of the tomb. But putting a guard on the tomb suggested it was not over yet.

15. The Cleft in the Rock

I find this narrative to be very intriguing. It is detailed in a book called <u>The Ark of the Covenant</u> by Jonathan Gray, a reputable Australian archaeologist and writer. I try to capture the main thread of his narrative, related to Mount Moriah.

"When Nebuchadnezzar sacked Jerusalem and destroyed the Temple in 586 BC, the Ark of the Covenant was not among the items seized. The Bible gives a list of things taken to Babylon, but the Ark is not included! The books of 2 Kings and Jeremiah give parallel inventories, which do not contradict each other in any way. And they make no mention of the Ark.

"Temple priests had evidently hidden them from the Babylonians. And at the restoration of the Temple some 70 years later, they would not be listed among the items brought back from Babylon to be reinstated in the Temple.

"In Jerusalem at the time, were some faithful men who determined to place beyond the reach of ruthless hands the sacred Ark containing the tablets of the Ten Commandments.

With mourning and sadness, they secreted the Ark in a cave. From that moment, the Ark was lost to history. Most Jewish legends agree that it was not destroyed or stolen, but hidden by God to await the end times. Several legends claim that the prophet Jeremiah was involved in hiding the Ark and other Temple treasures. It is not unreasonable to conclude that Jewish priests secretly hid it at the instigation of Jeremiah the prophet.

"It was commonly held by the ancient rabbis that the Ark would be found at the coming of the messiah."

The narrative goes on like this... In chapter 9 of the <u>Book of Daniel</u>, a prophecy is made about "70 weeks." That is 490 days. The year-for-a-day principle appears in Numbers 14:34 as a divinely established identity in prophetic symbolism; as also in Ezekiel 4:4-6 — "I have appointed thee each day for a year."So, the prophecy would be fulfilled 490 years after the decree of Artaxerxes to rebuild Jerusalem. This followed two earlier decrees by Cyrus and Darius that related only to the rebuilding of the

Temple (the second temple, at the time of Ezra). The third decree to restore the city (at the time of Nehemiah) starts the 490 years counting. This was in 457 BC, in the seventh year of the reign of Artaxerxes. He was the patron of Nehemiah's reconstruction project.

490 years after this starting point, if you do the math, is 33 AD. Daniel created the expectation that the "anointed one" or "messiah" would appear at that time. All the different strands of Judaism were expecting him around that time. The Gospels do not give dates, but they do capture the expectation and even excitement that a messiah had been promised. After all, it was Daniel whose strong witness in Babylon had caused the turn-around in imperial policy. His obedience to Yahweh was such a contrast to the disobedience that led to the Babylonian captivity in the first place!

It was around 33 AD that Yeshua (a k a Joshua or Jesus), son of Mary and raised in the home of Joseph Panther in Nazareth, entered the synagogue to proclaim: "The Spirit of the Lord is upon me, because he hath anointed me."

Luke's Gospel takes another run at this. He records that John the Baptist started his ministry "in the fifteenth year of the reign of Tiberius Caesar, Pontius Pilate being governor of Judaea, and Herod being tetrarch of Ituraea and of the region of Trachonitis, and Lysanius the tetrarch of Abilene, Annas and Caiaphas being the high priests..."

According to the Roman calendar, Tiberius commenced reigning on August 19, 14 AD. So, the fifteenth year of his reign would be 27 AD. The timing is very close. John went on to baptize Jesus at the beginning of his public ministry. Although exact dates are still debated (for example, how counting 490 years works at year zero? !), this is really why Jesus was accepted by so many Jews as the Messiah. They knew the "clues." The conversion of Gentiles would follow later, although Jesus himself never excluded them in his ministry.

The Synoptic Gospels indicate that the public ministry of Jesus was preceded by a public ministry of John, after which it lasted over three years. Daniel had prophesied that the life of the messiah would be "cut off" – implying a violent death.

Another prophet - Isaiah - spoke in similar terms in his prophesies of a coming Son of Man." The government would be upon his shoulder" ... he will be "despised and rejected of men"... "stricken"... "wounded"... "bruised"... "brought as a lamb to the slaughter"..."taken from prison and from judgment."

Daniel's prophecy includes this startling comment on the last week (i. e. the last year): "In the midst of the week he shall cause the sacrifice and the oblation to cease. "This is where the narrative gets really intriguing... how did this come to pass?

Yeshua was a faith-healer as well as a brilliant teacher. Socrates taught for 40 years, Aristotle for 40, Plato for 50 - and Yeshua for only three! Yet his parables compete with Lao Tzu and Aesop for universal wisdom and influence.

As Judaism was enthusiastically expecting a messiah, the Romans were very jumpy. So, when someone in society became very popular, this tended to threaten the Jewish religious leaders and worry the Roman military rulers. The miracles that Yeshua performed tended to enhance his popularity – even though he consistently asked people not to identify him. He seems to have understood the risks of populism.

On this note, Yeshua was well-versed in the Jewish scriptures – so he seems to have been well aware of prophesies of the anointed one and the Son of Man. According to the Gospels, which have proven time and again to be reliable sources, he did claim quite explicitly that it was him on the eve of Passover. He made no bones about it. And as he headed for Jerusalem on the fateful Passover, he did not shy away from where things were going. He stopped in Bethany on the way, where on his previous visit he had learned that a dear friend had died. The weeping and wailing of Lazarus' sisters was just too much for him. He wept. Then he raised Lazarus from his grave. This rocked public opinion to its foundations – the "jungle telegraph" (so to speak) went ballistic. He was greeted with huge acclaim as he entered the city. But this was just one bridge too far for the alliance of religious and military leaders. He had to be taken out.

He was betrayed. He was framed. Then they took him to Skull Hill to execute him, along with two common criminals. Mark 15:22 - "And they bring him unto the place *Golgotha*, which is, being interpreted, the place of a skull." Mark often slips into the historical present tense like he does there. It adds to the authenticity and drama of his telling.

Yeshua was crucified under Pontius Pilate, who was the Roman administrator ("procurator") of Judea between the years 26 and 36. The moment is the feast of Passover, very symbolic indeed. Yeshua celebrated the Seder or Passover supper with his inner circle on the eve that he was betrayed. Even before he was arrested, he instituted new meanings to the bread and wine – his body and his blood. He knew where this was going.

The place is at Calvary, on Mount Moriah, just outside Jerusalem. Now comes the *coup de grace* – the link between the crucifixion of Yeshua and the Ark of the Covenant (with the Mercy Seat mounted on top of it).

Passover lambs were always killed in the first month (Nisan), on the 14th day, "between the two evenings", which was the 9th hour of daylight. According to the first century Jewish historian Josephus, it was the custom in his day to offer the sacrifice at "about the ninth hour "or 3 p. m. Yeshua was lifted up onto the cross at Skull Hill around the third hour of daylight, at 9 a. m. He died six hours later, at 3p. m. Some signs and wonders were recorded at this moment of history, both in the Gospels and in extra-biblical sources as well. Starting with an eclipse of the sun at noon followed by an earthquake mid-afternoon.

Now archaeologists have been looking for the Ark of the Covenant for a long time. Jonathan Gray explores diverse narratives that have emerged over the centuries, as to where it landed – containing the two tablets with the Ten Commandments in God's handwriting. The motion picture Raiders of the Lost Ark popularized this quest. Gray describes a discovery that the goes something like this... The Ark was hidden in a cave in Mount Moria (outside the city wall) just before the Babylonians sacked Jerusalem. The prophet Jeremiah may have been involved? The Ark has not emerged since – it was never brought back to the second Temple. So, it was not carried off to either Babylon or to Rome after Titus decimated Jerusalem in 70 AD. It remained - and remains- hidden.

Calvary, Golgotha and Skull Hill are different names for one and the same place – an execution site outside the city wall. That was where the execution of Yeshua took place. Old Jerusalem straddles two summits – Mount Moria and Mount Zion. Calvary was on Mount Moriah. Excavations involving Jonathan Gray and his team discovered the cave where the Ark is hidden, in recent decades. It is below Skull Hill, and there is an ancient cleft in the rock above it. Gray reckons that the cleft in the rock was caused by the earthquake that is recorded both in the Gospels and in extra-biblical sources on Good Friday afternoon. His intriguing narrative is that the blood of Jesus actually dripped down onto the bedrock that his cross was anchored in, then down through the cleft in the rock into the cave. His blood dripped onto the Mercy Seat about six meters below -as a full and final propitiation for our sins. No more sacrifices were ever needed after that.

I am summarizing in dozens of lines what Gray writes in hundreds of pages – sprinkled with photos. I like the symbolism of this narrative. All is well, all is well with my soul.

I am not arguing from archaeology – I refer you to Jonathan Gray's book. He goes on to look for the tomb and again I can only commend his book to the reader. The symbolism and symmetry of this narrative is what I like – Yeshua gave his life (no one took it from him, <u>he gave it</u>) to save us. Here again are some lines directly from Jonathan Gray's book. He is a technical expert on archaeology, but he is an interpreter as well:

"Jesus gave one final cry with a loud voice, "Father, I commit my spirit into Your hands."As he submitted himself, the sense of the loss of his Father's favor was withdrawn. By faith, Jesus was victor. He had now become conscious of triumph and confident of his own resurrection.

"Immediately a fearful rumbling sound erupted from deep down m the earth. The ground shook violently and the rocks were split open. Jesus was dead.

"From the startled Roman centurion were forced the words, 'Truly this man was the Son of God."

Death by crucifixion was a slow process. A victim could linger on for days. Those soldiers were a special dispatch assigned to crucifixions. They were familiar with crucifixion scenes. They were shocked that Yeshua was dead already.

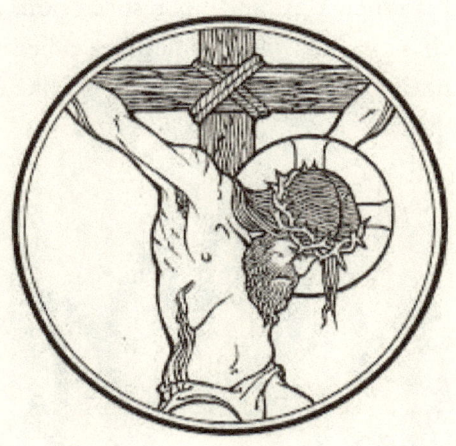

Lamb of God, who takes away the sins of the world, have mercy on us.

16. Black Saturday

"Low in the grave he lay, Jesus my Saviour
Waiting the coming day, Jesus my Lord"

Not much happened on this day, because it was the Sabbath, so not much could happen. On earth, that is.

But between his crucifixion and his resurrection, according to the creeds, "he descended into hell." It is sometimes called the harrowing of hell. Now, is that like a harrowing experience? Or like a farmer running his harrows over a field?

Well, the word "hell" combines several notions including "sheol" (Hebrew), "gehenna" (Latin), purgatory and also the bosom of Abraham. So, its "harrowing" or despoiling was because he robbed the afterlife of those who had been waiting "in limbo" for death to be defeated. Their souls were finally liberated and could start their journeys back to God, from whence they came.

As I understand orthodox theology, the soul connects with the body at the moment of conception. That is not just the connection of an "x" chromosome with a "y" chromosome but of a third element as well –

the soul, a little piece of God. Imago Dei. These physical and spiritual elements remain fused through gestation, birth and life. They only part at death, when the soul starts its journey back to God, just as the body is returned to dust and ashes.

But souls can get tainted through this connection, so they need purging or cleansing. That is where the notion of "purgatory" comes from. But a soul washed in the blood of Jesus may not need any further purging. Most of our souls have waited or will wait long periods of time to be reconnected with their bodies on the Day of Resurrection. For Jesus, this was just a short period because the Holy Spirit of God reconnected all his physical and spiritual elements in his victory over death. Therein is our hope of resurrection, in due course, while our souls "sleep" in eternity, out of time. But for those of us who are still trapped in time, the soul of Jesus was separated from his body on Black Saturday.

He descended into hell. He robbed hell of the souls who were waiting there in the underworld or afterlife for his victory over death. Then his soul was reconnected with his body and he came back to life. The same thing will happen to us, if we are part of his Body. Our souls may be parted from our bodies like his were, but we can count on their re-fusion on the Day of Resurrection because of his victory over death. But he needed to descend into hell to rob or harrow those who were there in waiting. The list was long - all the way back to Adam. "As in Adam all die, so also in Christ all shall be made alive. "

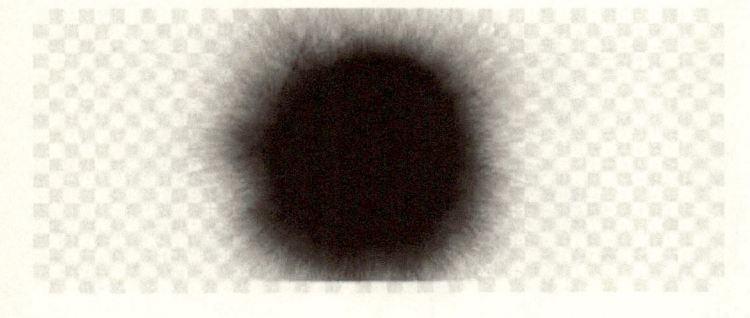

Here are the words of Christ to our first father, Adam: *"Out of love for you and for your descendants I now by my own authority command all who are held in bondage to come forth, all who are in darkness to be enlightened, all who are sleeping to arise. I order you, O sleeper, to awake. I did not create you to be held a prisoner in hell. Rise from the dead, for I am the life of the dead. Rise up, work of my hands, you who were created in my image. Rise, let us leave this place, for you are in me and I am in you; together we form only one person and we cannot be separated."*

17. Easter Sunday

I really shouldn't do this! It's too long, and it is one whole chapter out of my book called <u>Papyrus Pen Pals</u>. It is chapter 13 out of 25 chapters. This book mixes fact and fiction. My reckoning is that it is 70 percent history and 30 percent fiction. But to my fellow climbers on this ascent I am going to go ahead and share it. Please keep it between us. It is one "codex" of 24 contained in the book, so the publisher shouldn't mind too much! (The book is sub-titled "A-Team Chats," A is for apostle.)This codex is from Mary of Bethany to Joanna Chuza, both of whom were generous to Jesus and his disciples.

<u>Dead Men Walkin'</u>
   Month of Nisan; eighteenth year of Tiberias
   Dearest Joanna
   I hope this Codex finds you well? I miss our ladies' get-togethers. Between the festivals and the political turmoil of late, it has been hard to fit these in.

This month I finished off that expensive nardin that I bought from you last year. I am writing to tell you about it, and share what I know of recent events. Only glimpses. The day that Rabbi Joshua was executed, I gave what I had left of the nardin to Mary of Magdala. That morning, she was distressed by his arrest and needed some spices to prepare for the worst.

Sometimes our diminished role as women – unfair as it is - allows us to keep in the background, out of the limelight. Over Passover, Mary Magdalene had guest-lodging in the city, and Salome Boanerges was staying at her son John's house in town. During their visit from the north, they were able to slip in and out of various episodes, as they unfolded, with some anonymity. It all unravelled so fast! Especially after his triumphant entry into Jerusalem on the first day of the week. But that seems to have triggered a plot born of revenge? Mobs are so unpredictable; they were cheering him one day and baying for his blood only a few days later.

I had already opened the alabaster jar that I bought from you, and used some of the nardin once before. So, I gave the rest of it to Mary Magdalene. She slipped it to Joseph and Nicodemus as they wrapped him in grave clothes for burial, just before sunset. That was my way of honouring him. It was the least I could do. They already had some portions of their own, and blended my nardin into the mix. By working together as a team, sharing our resources, we can accomplish so much.

Come to think of it, the first time that I opened that alabaster jar was to give him a foot massage, when he was staying with us once before. That caused quite a stir! Some said that the ointment could have been sold to raise funds for the poor! When that critique of what I had done surfaced, I could feel the tensions of co-existing political views among the disciples. They were palpable. Some are very pro-poor and quite militant about it. While others seem to see that affluent people like ourselves have a contribution to make. And we have... we do!

Your import/export business is an example. You are well-placed for such a trade given your husband Chuza's procurement duties as Herod's steward. What a contact list you must have? And from so many places! That ointment from the Far East was expensive, but when you showed it to me, I must confess that something moved in my spirit and I had to buy it! I didn't know why at the time, but the intuitive impulse proved right. Twice I blessed my dear friend with it, no – I should say my dear Lord. For his victory over death has made us realize that he was like no other. He was no ordinary Rabbi or prophet.

At the time that I first cracked open that jar, he defended my aromatherapy as an extravagance that was my own special way of blessing him. When the debate over whether it was used properly died down, he did add something about keeping the rest of it for his burial. But only now am I connecting the dots.

Of course, we knew about his awesome powers when he raised my brother Lazarus from four days in the tomb. That was spectacular! But I think that among his critics, it generated more heat than light. They didn't like the way this inclined the mobs in his favour.

That was a day that I will never forget. We woke up still so heart-broken that morning, having buried our brother only days earlier. Martha and I had kept saying to one another that it would have never happened if Rabbi Joshua was here. In fact, that's how we greeted him – by wailing that if he had only been here, he could have saved Lazarus.

I always knew that he and my brother were bosom buddies, but to see him weep at the news of his death was moving. Then we took him to the tomb, as part of the grieving process. I was so startled when he called out: "Lazarus, come forth!" It was positively spooky. But then came a moment when joy and terror competed for my heart. My brother suddenly emerged from the tomb. He had trouble walking, because of those white linens that corpses are wrapped in for burial. Martha was quintessentially there first, un-wrapping him. Others joined her. Even the smells were mixed – the fragrance of burial spices with the odours of decomposition coming out of the tomb.

News of his command over death spread like wildfire on a windy day, through our village of Bethany and beyond. The crowd kept getting bigger and bigger. We rarely ever ask people to leave, for that is contrary to our code of hospitality. But on that day, we kept thanking people for dropping by, and in the next breath asking them to give us some space for grace.

After that day, I was of two minds. Would he use those powers that he could deploy at times to take on our oppressors by force? Or were those powers only to help others, not to save himself? That would be consistent with his teachings and practice. The reason that he enjoyed our hospitality and the comforts of our home so much, is that his visits punctuated a life of simplicity and at times self-denial. He was not an ascetic per se, but would spend periods fasting and praying. That was what his authenticity stemmed from. He could enjoy and be thankful when people shared with him the best things in life, but he was not ambitious for them. His focus was on "the other." He was a truly humble servant in this respect. A servant king.

I got my answer to this when they arrested him. I heard that they sent quite a posse to arrest him! They obviously knew that he had the powers to take them on. But when Peter snafued a sword from one of the guards and smacked him on the side of the head, cutting off his ear, Rabbi Joshua said that those who live by the sword will die by the sword. He picked up that severed ear off the ground and placed it back where it came from.

But when they laid him in Joseph of Arimathea's tomb after the execution, who was left to call out to him, like he had called out to Lazarus? "Come forth!" Mary Magdalene shared the Sabbath supper with us later that night, she was hardly coping. So, I went to sleep wondering what would happen next?

The week's events had taken their toll on all of us in different ways, although no one had suffered like him. Over the Sabbath we were paralysed with fear and expectancy. What would happen next?

Then Alphaeus arrived with his wife Mary. Jerusalem was full to capacity with the Passover crowd, and their lodging had expired. They had not planned to stay so long when they booked in. Events had taken a sudden turn for the worst, and they – like Joseph of Arimathea - were Rabbi Joshua's relatives. They could only improvise. So, we fit them in, and after settling in,

Mary Alphaeus made plans with Mary Magdalene and Salome Boanerges to go to the tomb before sunrise. I don't think they knew what to expect, as a Roman guard had been posted at the tomb. There had been an eclipse that darkened the afternoon sky on that Friday, and there was also an earthquake the night after the Sabbath. No one seemed to know where all these strange events were going.

The three ladies arrived there just before dawn. They found the stone rolled away and the tomb empty. The guard had left, probably spooked by the earthquake. Just the white linens, neatly folded where his body had been laid. They assumed that his body had been robbed, so Mary Magdalene took off in a tear to find Peter bar Jona and John Boanerges, where they were staying. As the sun rose, John arrived first at the tomb, running ahead of Peter. Someone else was there and reminded him that Rabbi Joshua had said to go back north, where he would rendezvous with them, in Galilee.

I promise you that if Martha and I had gone that morning, or even Lazarus, we would have immediately thought of resurrection. Because we once experienced it in our own lives, in our own family. But it took a while to sink in. First, they thought of grave-robbers! Then John Boanerges got it, according to his mom Salome who was there too. The pennies dropped.

Then Mary Magdalene actually met the risen Lord, walking around the garden. I remember Lazarus asking us questions about things that has happened while he lay in the tomb. It seems that Rabbi Joshua was getting his bearings back, like that, at the crack of dawn. He startled her. She thought it was the gardener, perhaps the bright morning sun was blinding her vision? But when he spoke to her, she recognized him, and she like John believed.

We rejoice that he is alive! We are so happy for him, and we ourselves are looking forward enthusiastically to being with him again.

Dear Joanna, that is all that I can tell you at present. We know that as a believer, you are in a tight spot with your husband's employment in Herod's court. But be not afraid. You have been chosen for a reason, and without you, there would have been no such precious nardin for his burial.

Keep in touch and thank you always for your generosity to our movement.

Your dear friend (and customer!)

Mary of Bethany

18. Epilogue

Do we live in the End Times? Will the Third Temple be constructed soon? It is very probable that the leaders of Judaism know where the Ark of the Covenant is. I hear that plans and finance for rebuilding the temple are already in place. It did not take French Catholics long to round up funding to rebuild Notre Dame Cathedral after the tragic fire in it. By the same token, funding a Third Temple should not be a problem.

However, there are many political issues blocking the way forward, including whether two monotheistic religions can share the same space on the citadel of Mount Moriah.

The end of the Seder of Passover supper ends with a toast "Next year in Jerusalem"! This can be metaphorical but for many people of faith it anticipates the real deal.

For Christians, faith has become global, not exclusive to the Jews but inclusive of the Gentiles as well. No matter whether Passover falls in springtime or harvest time, in the North or in the global South (which now boasts more Christians than the North), in the Catholic communion or among Protestants, we look forward to the return of Yeshua.

Even so, come, Lord Jesus!

About the Publisher

Mbokodo Publishers is your choice service provider and partner in the publishing business. We make your business our business in order to understand your needs, tastes and challenges better so we could provide you with the most efficient services imaginable.

Our professional and committed staff and personnel are always ready to assist you whenever you contact us. So drop us an email or simply call or visit our offices and this could be the beginning of a positive change in your life!

We look forward to being of ultimate assistance to you our dear prospective clients. For more information with regards to our offered products and services, please email us, mbokodopublishers@gmail.com

We look forward to hearing from you soon. God bless you!

Regards,

Publisher